INSPiRE

CHRISTIAN PULISIC

BY JOE TISCHLER

AMICUS LEARNING

Inspire is published by
Amicus Learning, an imprint of Amicus
P.O. Box 227
Mankato, MN 56002
www.amicuspublishing.us

Editor: Aidan Whitcomb and Megan Siewert
Series Designer: Kathleen Petelinsek
Book Designer: Grant Gould

Library of Congress Cataloging-in-Publication Data
Names: Tischler, Joe, author.
Title: Christian Pulisic / by Joe Tischler.
Description: Mankato, MN : Amicus Learning, [2025] | Series: Inspire | Includes bibliographical references and index. | Audience: Ages 5–9 | Audience: Grades 2–3 | Summary: "Learn about World Cup superstar Christian Pulisic and his accomplishments in soccer in this biography packed with action photos and fact-filled text suitable for young readers. Includes table of contents, glossary, further resources, and index"—Provided by publisher.
Identifiers: LCCN 2023046007 (print) | LCCN 2023046008 (ebook) | ISBN 9781645499060 (library binding) | ISBN 9781645499145 (paperback) | ISBN 9781645499220 (ebook)
Subjects: LCSH: Pulisic, Christian, 1998- —Juvenile literature. | Soccer players—United States—Biography—Juvenile literature.
Classification: LCC GV942.7.P84 T57 2025 (print) | LCC GV942.7.P84 (ebook) | DDC 796.334092 [B]—dc23/eng/20231019
LC record available at https://lccn.loc.gov/2023046007
LC ebook record available at https://lccn.loc.gov/2023046008

Photo Credits: Alamy/Greg Balfour Evans, 8–9; AP Newsroom/Robin Alam, Cover; Getty/Alessandro Sabattini, 20–21, Brad Smith, 5, Chris Lee-Chelsea FC, 14, Darren Walsh, 6–7, John Dorton, 16–17, 18, Robin Alam, 13, Shaun Botterill, 15, TF-Images, 10; Shutterstock/Photo Melon, 7, Poetra.RH, 12

Printed in China

Table of Contents

4 Soccer Star
7 Soccer Family
8 Youth Start
11 Off to Germany
12 National Team
15 Club Success
16 Captain America
19 Scoring and Assisting
20 Team Player
22 Super Stats
23 Glossary
24 Read More
24 On the Web
24 Index

Soccer Star

Christian Pulisic dribbles across the **pitch**. He sees an opening. He kicks hard with his right foot. GOAL!

Pulisic is one of the best soccer players in the world. He plays for the United States Men's National Team (USMNT) and A.C. Milan.

Pulisic is on his way to becoming one of the greatest American born soccer players of all time.

Both of Pulisic's parents have supported his soccer playing since he was young.

Soccer Family

Pulisic was born in Hershey, Pennsylvania. He comes from a soccer-playing family. His parents played in college. They went to George Mason University in Virginia. His father played professional indoor soccer.

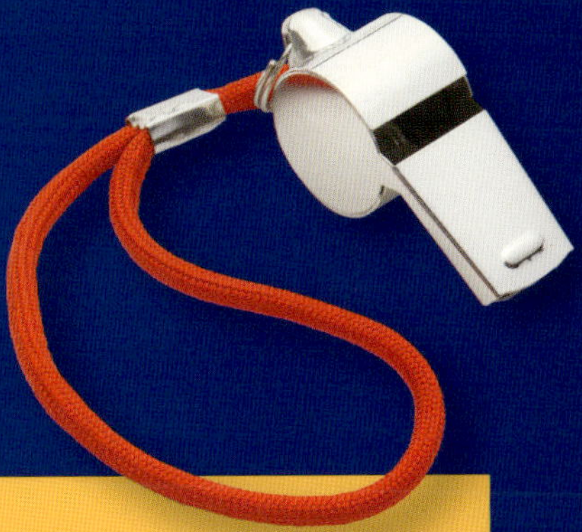

COACH DAD

Pulisic's father was a soccer coach. He coached college teams and youth teams.

Youth Start

Pulisic moved around a lot as a child. His family spent a year in England. He played for the Brackley Town youth team. That was his first time playing for a team in Europe. The family later moved to Michigan. He played for another youth team there.

The town of Brackley, England is well known for the Brackley Town youth soccer team.

Moving to Germany let Pulisic get the experience he needed to become the great player he is today.

Off to Germany

Pulisic moved to Germany in 2014. A club team, Borussia Dortmund, signed him. He was just 16 years old. He played for the under-17 (U17) team at first. He scored many goals. He was called up to the senior team a year later.

National Team

In soccer, players can also play for their **national team**. In 2016, Pulisic played his first game for the USMNT. He was the youngest player to play for the United States in a World Cup qualifying match. He later became the youngest USMNT player to score a goal.

A NATIONAL STAGE

Pulisic was just 17 years, 193 days old when he made his USMNT start.

Pulisic battles for control of the ball in a game against the Mexico Men's National Team.

Pulisic catches the ball in midair.

Club Success

Pulisic changed club teams in 2019. He went to Chelsea in the English Premier League. It's the top league in England. He scored a **hat trick** in his first season. He is the youngest player to do so for Chelsea.

SCORING GOALS
Pulisic scored 26 goals with Chelsea. He helped them win the Champions League in 2021.

Pulisic is one of the youngest players ever to captain the USMNT.

Captain America

The USMNT earned a spot at the 2022 FIFA World Cup. Pulisic is a **team captain**. Through 2023, he has 28 goals for the USMNT. He also has 15 assists. He will be one of the key players for the USMNT at the 2026 World Cup.

NICKNAME
Pulisic is nicknamed "Captain America." That's a superhero from Marvel Comics.

2
10
21

Pulisic quickly steals the ball from a Netherlands player in the 2022 FIFA World Cup.

Scoring and Assisting

At the 2022 FIFA World Cup, Pulisic scored or assisted on all USMNT goals. His goal against Iran moved the team on to the **knockout round**. He earned two "Man of the Match" awards during the Cup.

Pulisic celebrates with a teammate after A.C. Milan scores a goal.

Team Player

Pulisic now plays for the club team A.C. Milan. It is in Italy. He scored a goal in his first game with the team. He is still captain of the USMNT, too. He is an important player for both teams. He hopes to lead them to many trophies in the future.

SUPER STATS

CHRISTIAN PULISIC

Born: September 18, 1998

Birthplace: Hershey, Pennsylvania

Current Teams: United States Men's National Team, A.C. Milan (Italian Serie A)

AWARDS/ACCOMPLISHMENTS

CONCACAF Nations League Player of the Tournament: 2022–23

UEFA Champions League champion: 2021

U.S. Soccer Male Athlete of the Year: 2017, 2019, 2021

GLOSSARY

hat trick The scoring of three goals in a game by one player.

knockout round A competition in which a losing team is eliminated right away.

national team A team made up of players all from the same country.

pitch Another term for a soccer field.

team captain A player who represents and leads the team both on and off the field.

READ MORE

Fishman, Jon M. **Christian Pulisic.** Minneapolis: Lerner Publications, 2022.

Kortemeier, Todd. **Christian Pulisic.** Minneapolis: SportsZone, Abdo Publishing, 2020.

Schoenherr, Charles. **Soccer Superstars.** Mankato, Minn.: The Child's World, 2022.

ON THE WEB

FIFA World Cup Facts for Kids
https://kids.kiddle.co/FIFA_World_Cup

USA Soccer
https://www.ussoccer.com/players/p/christian-pulisic

INDEX

A.C. Milan, 4, 21
assists, 16, 19
Borussia Dortmund, 11
captain, 16, 21
Champions League, 15
Chelsea, 15
family, 7
hat trick, 15
USMNT, 4, 12, 16, 19, 21
World Cup, 12, 16, 19

About the Author

Joe Tischler is an editor, sports journalist, and avid sports fan living in Minnesota. He has written about high school, collegiate, and professional games for newspapers. His favorite teams are the Twins, Vikings, Timberwolves, and Golden Gophers.